Awesome
Animal
Skills

Cougars and Other Animals That Ambush Prey

Vic Kovacs

WINDMILL
BOOKS

New York

Published in 2016 by **Windmill Books**,
an Imprint of Rosen Publishing
29 East 21st Street, New York, NY 10010

Developed and produced for Rosen by BlueAppleWorks Inc.

Art Director: T.J. Choleva
Managing Editor for BlueAppleWorks: Melissa McClellan
Designer: Joshua Avramson
Photo Research: Jane Reid
Editor: Marcia Abramson

Photo Credits:
Cover Scott E Read/Shutterstock; back cover, p. 22 Dennis van de Water/Shutterstock; title page Seread/Dreamstime; TOC top Ewa Studio/Shutterstock;
TOC bottom Artush/Thinkstock; p. 4 top left Alta Oosthuizen/Shutterstock; p. 4 top, 20 top, 20, 22 top Cathy Keifer/Shutterstock; p.4-5, 10 Outdoorsman/
Dreamstime; p. 6 top left Design Pics/Thinkstock; p. 6 top, 8 bottom Mikael Males/Dreamstime; p. 6 left Catherine Downie/Dreamstime; p. 6 Sally Wallis/
Dreamstime; p. 7 JohnPitcher/Thinkstock; p. 8 top left, 8 top Jupiterimages/Thinkstock; p. 8-9, 10 top Tom Brakefield/Thinkstock; p. 9 top Marques/
Shutterstock; p. 10-11 Tony Rix/Shutterstock; p. 11 Tom Reichner/Shutterstock; p. 12 top left Volt Collection/Shutterstock; p. 12 top Doethion/Dreamstime;
p. 12 middle Kuipersa/Dreamstime; p. 12 bottom, 13 top, 13 Dmytro Pylypenko/Dreamstime; p. 14 top left Marietjie/Shutterstock; p. 14 top Anup
Shah/Thinkstock; p. 14, 27 Hxdbzxy/Dreamstime; p. 14 right Hedrus/Dreamstime; p. 15 Sergey Uryadnikov/Shutterstock; p. 15 right Stephen Noakes/
Shutterstock; p. 16 top left Steve Childs/Creative Commons; p. 16 top Starfield/Dreamstime; p. 16 bottom Kasparart/Dreamstime; p. 16-17 Ethan Daniels/
Shutterstock; p. 17 right Claudio Dias/Shutterstock; p. 18 top left BrianLasenby/Thinkstock; p. 18 top alexeys/Thinkstock; p. 18 FloridaStock/Shutterstock;
p. 18 bottom right Tory Kallman/Shutterstock; p. 19, 19 right Heikki Mäkikallio/Dreamstime; p. 20 top left francesco de marco/Shutterstock; p. 21 Dr. Morley
Read/Shutterstock; p. 21 right nattrass/Thinkstock; p. 22 top left Gaschwald/Shutterstock; p. 22 left Chantelle Bosch/Shutterstock; p. 23 Svoboda Pavel/
Shutterstock; p. 23 right Miloslav Doubrava/Dreamstime; p. 24 top left David Byron Keener/Shutterstock; p. 24 top Steve Byland/Shutterstock; p. 24-25
Brykaylo Yuriy/Shutterstock; p. 24 right Wildphoto3/Shutterstock; p. 25 left Dario Sanches/Creative Commons; p. 25 Mike Trewet/Dreamstime; p. 25 right
U.S. Fish and Wildlife Service/Creative Commons; p. 26 top left lightberserk/Shutterstock; p. 26 top dickysingh/Thinkstock; p. 26 left Stef Maruch/Creative
Commons; p. 26 MaZiKab/Thinkstock; p. 27 right Fei Han/Dreamstime; p. 28 top left Reinhold Leitner/Shutterstock; p. 28 top Utopia_88/Thinkstock; p. 28
left Morris Mann/Shutterstock; p. 28-29, 29 right JedsPics_com/Thinkstock.

Cataloging-in-Publication-Data

Kovacs, Vic.
Cougars and other animals that ambush prey / by Vic Kovacs.
p. cm. — (Awesome animal skills)
Includes index.
ISBN 978-1-4777-5649-2 (pbk.)
ISBN 978-1-4777-5648-5 (6 pack)
ISBN 978-1-4777-5580-8 (library binding)
1. Cougar — Juvenile literature. 2. Animal behavior — Juvenile literature.
3. Predatory animals — Juvenile literature. I. Title.
QL737.C23 K68 2016
599.75'24—d23

Manufactured in the United States of America

CPSIA Compliance Information: Batch #WS15WM: For Further Information contact: Rosen Publishing, New York, New York at 1-800-237-9932

CONTENTS

HUNTING AMBUSH STYLE

Surprise! That's the name of the game in an ambush, where **predators** lie in wait to attack their **prey.** They usually stay hidden until the last moment, then spring upon their unsuspecting prey. Ambushers use the sit-and-wait style of hunting because their bodies are more suited to short bursts of speed than long chases. This helps them catch up with rapidly moving prey. An element of **camouflage** is often involved, too. Ambush predators include many fish, snakes, and other reptiles, as well as some mammals, birds, insects, and spiders.

A cougar kitten practices hunting. Learning from their mother, kittens start with small prey such as rabbits.

SNEAKY HUNTERS

An ambush predator will wait, often for a long time, for prey to come near. Ambush tactics can include hiding in tree branches, **coiling** up amid leaves, blending in with the nearby rocks and foliage, or swooping down from ledges. Staying very still and in most cases, demonstrating amazing patience, are two other tactics shared by ambush predators.

DID YOU KNOW?

By sitting and waiting for prey, the ambush predator makes efficient use of its energy, which helps it survive.

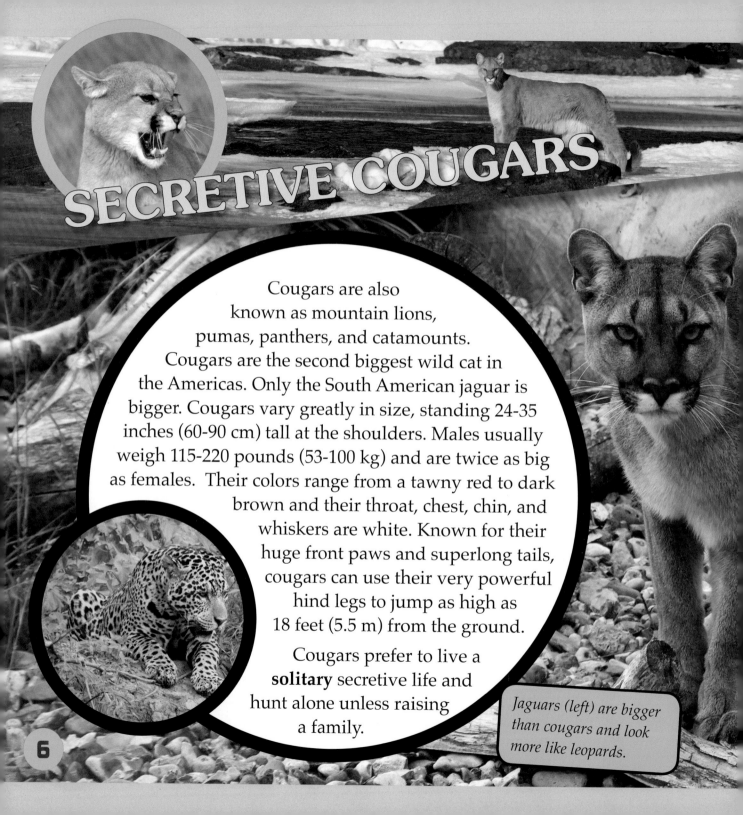

Cougars are also known as mountain lions, pumas, panthers, and catamounts. Cougars are the second biggest wild cat in the Americas. Only the South American jaguar is bigger. Cougars vary greatly in size, standing 24-35 inches (60-90 cm) tall at the shoulders. Males usually weigh 115-220 pounds (53-100 kg) and are twice as big as females. Their colors range from a tawny red to dark brown and their throat, chest, chin, and whiskers are white. Known for their huge front paws and superlong tails, cougars can use their very powerful hind legs to jump as high as 18 feet (5.5 m) from the ground.

Cougars prefer to live a **solitary** secretive life and hunt alone unless raising a family.

Jaguars (left) are bigger than cougars and look more like leopards.

Cougars are called "catamounts" in the New England area of the United States. It is probably short for "cat of the mountains." Cougars do look cat-like. They are more closely related to house cats than to tigers or jaguars.

Cougars are good climbers. They often hide in trees to wait for prey.

NIGHT HUNTERS

Cougars are **carnivores**, feeding almost entirely on meat. Their main meal of choice is elk and deer, but they will also eat mice, beavers, porcupines, raccoons, and hares. Their prey can be as small as insects and birds and as large as moose and cattle.

That is a lot of prey, but cougars must compete for it with the gray wolves that live in the same areas. Wolves may fight to take a cougar's kill or even prey on small cougars. Like a cat, cougars may climb a tree to escape! They also are good swimmers.

Wolves usually win their fights over prey with cougars, but not always, biologists have discovered.

NIGHT PROWLERS

These **notorious** hunters live in dark, dense forest dens, beneath uprooted trees, and on rocky mountain ledges. Being **nocturnal** animals they mostly hunt from dawn till dusk, although sightings during daylight hours do occur. Cougars may go long distances as they seek prey. They can run as fast as 40-50 miles per hour (64-80 km/h) but they tend to save that speed for short bursts as they pounce. A cougar can kill prey four times its size because of its powerful, muscular build and quiet, **stealthy** ways.

Cougars have powerful jaws and sharp teeth for bringing down and cutting up prey.

LEARNED HUNTING SKILLS

Mother cougars give birth to litters of one to six kittens in dens that are hidden for protection. The mother raises the kittens alone. When they are about two months old, she starts teaching them to ambush prey. By the time they are six months old, they have stopped nursing and can hunt small prey by themselves. They will be ready to go out on their own when they are about two years old.

Cougars are born with brown fur, black spots, and black bars on their tails. After six months, the spots are barely visible.

IN ACTION

Cougars first stalk their prey for some distance. They then tackle their targeted meal by leaping onto their backs and forcing them to the ground. With razor-sharp teeth they cut through the necks and throats of their **quarry**, strangling them to death. Sometimes they even use their claws to rake the deer or elk in order to cripple it. A cougar kills approximately one deer or elk every two weeks and will consume about eight pounds (3.6 kg) of meat in one sitting before hiding the rest under sticks and leaves. All told, a cougar eats about three-quarters of its kill, wasting very little of its hard-earned meal.

Cougars use vegetation, rocks, and slopes for cover so they can surprise their prey.

PATIENT LEOPARD SEALS

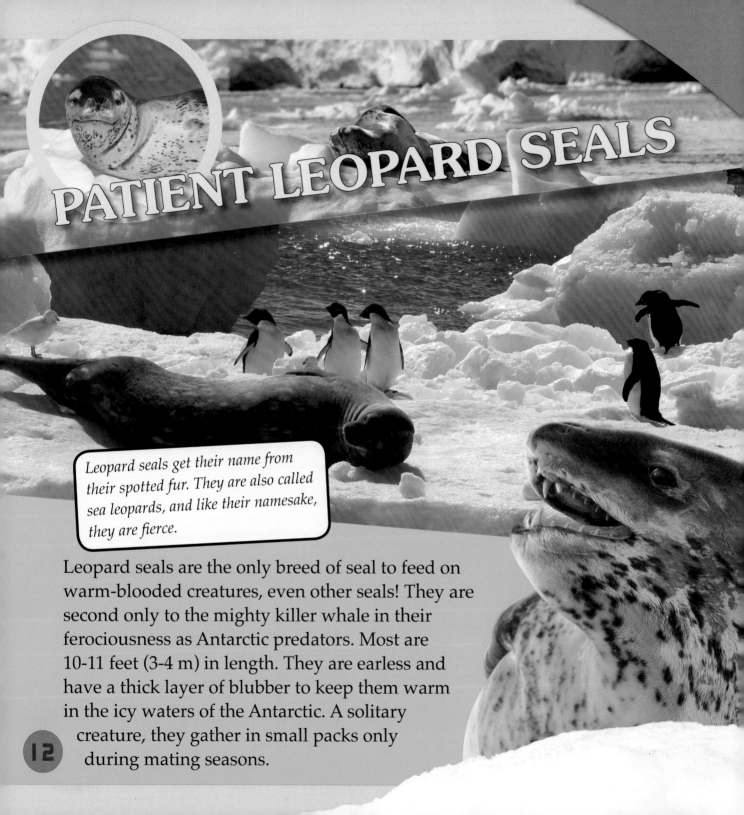

> Leopard seals get their name from their spotted fur. They are also called sea leopards, and like their namesake, they are fierce.

Leopard seals are the only breed of seal to feed on warm-blooded creatures, even other seals! They are second only to the mighty killer whale in their ferociousness as Antarctic predators. Most are 10-11 feet (3-4 m) in length. They are earless and have a thick layer of blubber to keep them warm in the icy waters of the Antarctic. A solitary creature, they gather in small packs only during mating seasons.

HUNTING SKILLS

Sea leopards dine on fish, shellfish, other seals, and squid. They also eat penguins. Waiting patiently underwater near an ice shelf, they snare the birds just as they enter the water. Sometimes they come up underneath seabirds resting on the ocean surface and snatch them in their jaws. At low tides, sea leopards will lie very still, blending in with the rocks, and will attack penguins from this camouflaged, flattened position. They often grab the penguins' feet and fling them back and forth, beating them against the surface of the water to kill them. It probably softens the meal as well, to add to the predators' enjoyment.

Leopard seals lurk near the surface of open water to wait for prey. They are so strong that they also can leap onto the ice to grab a meal.

QUICK CROCODILES

There are thirteen species of crocodiles. The dwarf crocodile is the smallest, at over 5 feet (1.5 m). The saltwater crocodile slithers in as king as the longest on record, coming in at more than 20 feet (6 m). That's more than three grown men stacked head to toe! Crocodiles inhabit hot areas in Africa, Asia, the Americas, and Australia. A special gland in their tongues enables them to tolerate salt.

As long as it's warm, they can live in freshwater or salt water. They are considered to be the most social of reptiles, and many species live in loose shoreline groupings. During feeding and **basking** times, all but the **territorial** saltwater crocodile will tolerate one another without serious conflict. Carnivores all the way, they feed on fish, birds, reptiles, and mammals.

Large crocodiles prey on large animals such as zebras, wildebeests, and antelopes, but they don't mind eating fish when available.

CAPTURED ON CAMERA

Crocodiles have perfected the art of the ambush. They lie in wait submerged at the river's edge for long periods of time, then rush their prey at the perfect moment when the prey is having a drink. Crocodiles are surprisingly fast in their attacks. Once they grab their prey in their powerful jaws there is no escape. The prey is usually killed by drowning or being torn apart.

15

DEVIOUS ANGLERFISH

Anglerfish get their name from the way they hunt. A long strand of their dorsal spine, with a fleshy knob at the end, sticks out from between their eyes. This is known as the **illicium**. Anglerfish wave the illicium around, using the knob as bait. They are carnivores, so they hunt for **crustaceans**, fish, and sometimes other anglerfish.

Biologists divide anglerfish into four groups called batfish, goosefish, frogfish, and deep-sea angler. Within the groups there are more than 200 species. Many live on the bottom of the sea. Deep-sea anglers can be found nearly a mile down.

On the ocean floor, frogfish use their specialized fins to move with a rocking or galloping **gait**.

The biggest deep-sea anglers are about 4 feet (1.2 m) long.

SUCKING IT IN

Frogfish rely on camouflage to snare prey. They have colors, shapes, and textures that allow them to blend in with rocks, coral, sponges, and algae. Some can even change color. They can be as small as an inch (2.5 cm) or as long as 15 inches (38 cm). They live in tropical and subtropical waters all over the word.

These patient hunters often wait in one spot for a long time for prey to come by. Their disguises help them evade predators, too. Once a hidden frogfish spots prey with its eyes, it waves its illicium around. As the prey swims near to get at the bait, the frogfish quickly gulps it up along with a mouthful of water. This may take less than six milliseconds!

A frogfish can expand its mouth and even its stomach to take in prey twice its size.

SHREWD GREEN HERONS

Green herons are named for the velvet-green feathers on their back. They have a dagger-like beat that they use to spear fish. They are about 17 inches (44 cm) long. That is about the size of a crow, which is small for a heron. Green herons live mostly in wetlands in North and Central America, where they usually hunt at dusk and dawn. Their green and brown coloring helps to camouflage them. They mostly eat small fish, but also dine on insects, spiders, snails, frogs, reptiles, and rodents.

Green herons are one of the few tool-using bird species. They can make a fishing lure from insects, earthworms, twigs, and even feathers. Green herons dangle these objects on the surface of the water to entice small fish.

SPEAR FISHING

Green herons hunt alone. They stand on a rock or twig with their bodies stretched out low, ready to grab prey out of shallow water or spear it with their beak.

They also hunt by wading into shallow water or even flying out into deep water, where they dive for larger prey. Webs on their feet help them with the long swim back to shore.

When very hungry or raising babies, green herons will hunt and dive for food all day long.

19

SPOOKY PRAYING MANTISES

Praying mantises are predatory insects that live in warm and tropical environments. They are named as such because their bent front legs resemble a typical prayer position. You might have seen one of these spooky creatures and not known it, because they blend in with the grass and weeds so well. Mantises are masters of camouflage, which they use to blend in with their surroundings to avoid predators and to better snare their prey. Moths, crickets, grasshoppers, flies, and other insects are usually dinner. However, these insects will also eat others of their own kind. The adult female, for example, sometimes eats her mate.

A praying mantis will sit quietly and time its attack, then strike with lightning speed. It has such quick reflexes that it can snatch a flying insect out of the air.

Two large eyes give the mantis great vision for hunting. It is the only insect that can look over its shoulder. A mantis can swivel its head 180 degrees.

EATING IT ALL

Praying mantises live in a state of ambush, staying very still until their prey wanders close enough. They will also stalk their desired meal, but usually the stock-still method works best. These predatory insects have reflexes so fast they can't be seen by the naked eye! What might look like a blade of grass is soon revealed to be a high-speed killer, but too late! Mantises use their spiked front legs to snare their prey and pin it in place. Then they apply their strong **mandibles**. If the prey resists, the mantis bites off its head to kill it, then chews it up. If the prey gives up, the mantis eats it alive. Either way, most of it will be eaten.

LIGHTNING-FAST CHAMELEONS

Chameleons can hunt with one eye and scan for danger with the other. Each eye rotates separately.

Chameleons are unique lizards known for their ability to change their color. There are nearly 160 species of chameleon. They live in many different habitats, from rain forests to deserts, in Africa, southern Europe, and across south Asia. Chameleons do not change their colors just to blend with the surroundings. Studies show that light, temperature, and even mood can cause chameleons to change color. Sometimes changing color just makes the chameleon more comfortable, or helps it to communicate with other chameleons.

QUICK TONGUES

Most chameleons spend their life in trees and bushes where they hunt mainly insects. Being an ambush predator, chameleons can wait for a very long time for prey to come by. When in range, chameleons use their long tongues to catch the prey. Their tongues are the same or double the length of their bodies, and can reach the prey at extremely high speed, in as little as 0.07 seconds. The chameleon tongue's tip is a **protruding** ball of muscle, and as it hits its prey it forms a small suction cup. Once the tongue smacks against the prey, it sticks tight. The tongue then slips back into the chameleon's open mouth with a yummy treat.

Chameleons are well adapted to living in trees. They have special toes for gripping branches so they can even sway in the wind. In addition, chameleons can wrap their tails around tree branches while climbing.

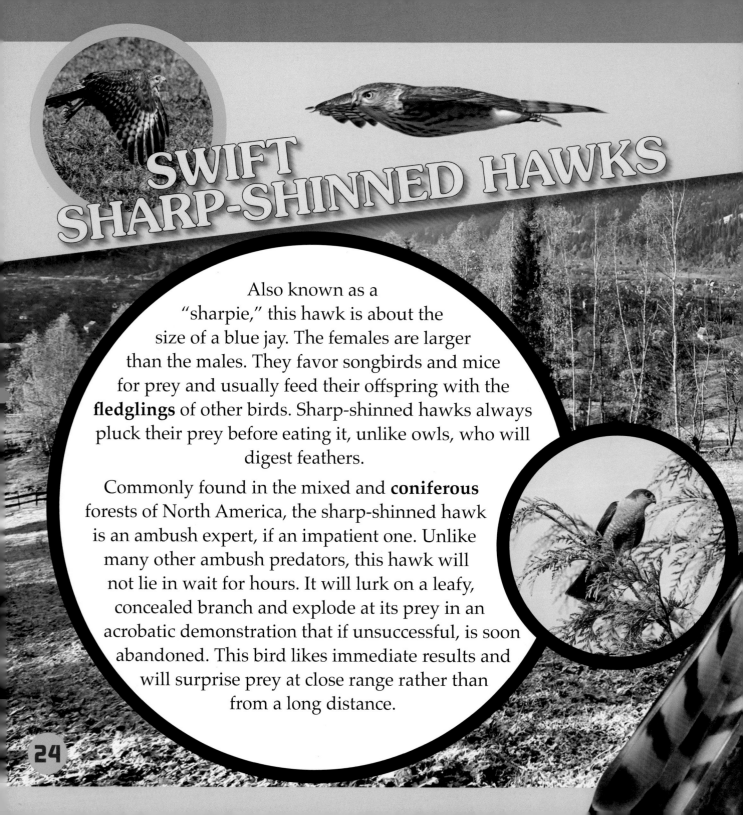

SWIFT SHARP-SHINNED HAWKS

Also known as a "sharpie," this hawk is about the size of a blue jay. The females are larger than the males. They favor songbirds and mice for prey and usually feed their offspring with the **fledglings** of other birds. Sharp-shinned hawks always pluck their prey before eating it, unlike owls, who will digest feathers.

Commonly found in the mixed and **coniferous** forests of North America, the sharp-shinned hawk is an ambush expert, if an impatient one. Unlike many other ambush predators, this hawk will not lie in wait for hours. It will lurk on a leafy, concealed branch and explode at its prey in an acrobatic demonstration that if unsuccessful, is soon abandoned. This bird likes immediate results and will surprise prey at close range rather than from a long distance.

Male sharp-shinned hawks are the smallest hawks in the United States and Canada.

Sharpies are fierce hunters with razor-sharp claws. They help to control wild bird populations.

WISE TIGERS

Tigers were chosen as the national animal of India and several other countries because of their power and beauty.

Tigers once roamed all of Asia, but less than 4,000 are left in the wild because of over-hunting and habitat destruction. They live in areas with lots of vegetation, water, and prey. Tigers eat large mammals such as deer and water buffalo. They often hide a big kill under vegetation so they can eat it over several days. Tigers belong to the cat family. They are the largest cat, too, weighing as much as 660 pounds (300 kg). Most have reddish coats with black, brown, or gray stripes for camouflage. A few are rare white tigers.

Tigers are good swimmers. They can swim long distances and catch prey in the water.

AMBUSHING THE PREY

Tigers will use a combination of stalking and lying in ambush to shock their prey, usually near a water source where the prey's defenses are down. They use their strength and massive body weight to knock prey to the ground, killing with a fatal bite to the neck. Holding its prey with its spread, large-clawed paws, the tiger stays latched onto the neck until its prey is strangled to death. Not exactly a loving embrace! Tigers have killed prey weighing almost six times as much as they do, such as a water buffalo. If potential prey looks too dangerous to handle, though, they stay away. They prefer to make an easy kill by hunting animals that are sick or weak.

SNEAKY PYTHONS

Pythons are among the world's largest nonvenomous snakes. They are found in Africa, Southeast Asia, and Australia. Most pythons live in the rugged underbrush of dense tropical rain forest regions. They are excellent climbers; some species, such as the green tree python, are arboreal and live in trees. Like all snakes, they are also very good swimmers, but they hunt mostly on land. They eat mammals, birds, reptiles, and amphibians. Bigger pythons go after bigger prey.

A green tree python will coil around a branch in a saddle-like shape when resting.

DEADLY HUGS

Most python species are ambush predators. They lie in a camouflaged location, waiting, then spring to attack when the prey is least suspecting a predator. An attacking python will use its sharp teeth to grasp the prey and then kill it by quickly coiling around it, slowly squeezing the prey to death. Pythons are constrictors. They coil themselves up around their prey, tightening and squeezing hard enough to stop the prey's breathing. They do not crush the prey completely as was once believed. Their prey is rarely visibly mangled before being swallowed. Pythons swallow all their prey whole and then retire to digest it. Fully digesting their prey may take several days or even weeks. That is one long after-lunch nap!

Huge, flexible jaws help the python swallow large prey.

GLOSSARY

BASKING Bathing in the sun, often on a shoreline but not always.

CAMOUFLAGE Colors, textures, or materials that help animals blend into their environment and escape notice.

CARNIVORE Meat eater.

COILING Winding into rings laid within or on top of each other or around an object.

CONIFEROUS Forests made up of pines, spruces, and firs.

CRUSTACEANS Shellfish; aquatic species with a segmented body and hard exoskeleton (shell) such as crabs, lobsters, etc.

FLEDGLINGS Newly hatched babies.

GAIT A way of walking or running, such as a gallop.

ILLICIUM Scientific name for the anglerfish's "fishing pole."

MANDIBLES The mouthparts of insects or arachnids used to bite or hold food.

NOCTURNAL Active at night.

NOTORIOUS Famous, often not in a good way.

PREDATOR Any animal that hunts and feeds on other animals.

PREY Any animal that is hunted and eaten by other animals.

PROTRUDING Sticking out.

QUARRY Another word for prey.

SOLITARY Alone, living independent of a group.

STEALTHY Sneaky and extremely quiet.

TERRITORIAL Possessive of an area or region.

FOR MORE INFORMATION

Further Reading

Burnie, David. *Predator*.
New York, NY: DK Publishing, 2011.

Hernandez, Christopher. *Animal Superpowers*.
New York, NY: Scholastic, 2012.

Jenkins, Steve. *The Animal Book: A Collection of the Fastest, Fiercest, Toughest, Cleverest, Shyest—and Most Surprising—Animals on Earth*.
Boston, MA: Houghton Mifflin Harcourt, 2013.

Person, Stephen. *Cougar: A Cat with Many Names*.
New York, NY: Bearport Publishing, 2012.

WEBSITES

For web resources related to the subject of this book, go to:
www.windmillbooks.com/weblinks and select this book's title.

INDEX